Postman Pc

Wild Cat Chase

Story by ***John Cunliffe***

Pictures by ***Ray Mutimer***

from the original Television designs by ***Ivor Wood***

Scholastic Children's Books,
Scholastic Publications Ltd,
7-9 Pratt Street, London NW1 OAE, UK

Scholastic Inc.,
555 Broadway, New York, NY 10012 – 3999, USA

Scholastic Canada Ltd,
123 Newkirk Road, Richmond Hill,
Ontario, Canada L4C 3G5

Ashton Scholastic Pty Ltd,
PO Box 579, Gosford, New South Wales,
Australia

Ashton Scholastic Ltd,
Private Bag 92801, Penrose, Auckland,
New Zealand

First published by Andre Deutsch Children's Books, an imprint of
Scholastic Publications Ltd 1992

ISBN: 0 590 55303 8

Printed by Proost International Book Production.

10 9 8 7 6 5 4 3 2 1

One fine day, Postman Pat called on Miss Hubbard with some letters. It was quiet in Miss Hubbard's garden. It was so quiet that Pat could hear the bees buzzing. Then he heard another sound.

"What's that?" said Pat.

He heard it again. *Clickety-click . . . clickety-click.*

Jess didn't know what it was. He was trying to hear a mouse, scratching in the wall. He had never met a mouse that went *clickety-click*.

When Pat walked round the corner, he knew what it was. It was Miss Hubbard sitting out in the sunshine with her knitting. Her needles went *clickety-click* and flashed in and out of the wool.

“My goodness,” said Pat, “I wish I could knit at that speed.”

“It all comes with practice,” said Miss Hubbard.

She set down her knitting to look at the letters that Pat had brought her.

Jess looked at her knitting. He didn't know what it was. It was bright orange and fluffy. A fluffy orange jumper. But Jess thought it might be a fluffy orange mouse. A big mouse, that said *clickety-click* instead of *squeak*! But now it was quiet. Perhaps it was asleep? Jess sat down in the grass, with his tail waving slowly to and fro, ready to spring.

"Now then, Jess," said Pat, "it's only wool."

But, before Pat could stop him, Jess sprang! He jumped on the knitting and put all his claws in it. He rolled over, fighting the knitting. The wool tangled in his claws. The wool wrapped round his paws and round his nose. The needles poked him.

Poor old Jess! It wasn't a mouse, it was a woolly monster! He thought it was going to gobble him up. So he up and ran for it.

Jess ran for his life across Miss Hubbard's garden. And the knitting chased after him. He didn't know he was pulling it with the wool that was tangled round his legs.

Jess ran out of the garden gate. He ran down the lane. Pat and Miss Hubbard ran after him. Faster, faster. No matter how fast Jess ran, the woolly monster kept up with him.

Ted came round the corner on his bike, just missed Jess and crashed into the prickly hedge. Then he jumped off and joined in the chase.

Jess did not stop. The knitting did not stop.

Jess ran into a field where Peter Fogg was feeding the hens. Jess ran right through the middle of the hens. They ran, clucking, in all directions. Peter shouted, "STOP!" The knitting knocked the bucket of hen-food over. Jess ran on. Peter joined in the chase.

Jess did not stop. The knitting did not stop.

Jess ran into the duck-pond at Greendale Farm. The knitting splashed through the water after him. Oh, what a noise the ducks made. Katy ran to close the gate, but Jess and the knitting squeezed through a hole in the hedge. Katy and Tom joined in the chase.

Jess did not stop. The knitting did not stop.

Jess ran into Mrs. Pottage's garden. He ran round the flower-beds. He ran round the sundial. He ran round the paddling-pool. The knitting still ran with him.

Poor Jess was getting tired. The knitting did not seem a bit tired. As long as Jess ran, the knitting ran after him.

Mrs. Pottage was in the garden, trimming the hedge with her shears. She knew just what to do. As Jess and the knitting ran past her, she went *snip*, with her shears, and snipped the long piece of wool that was pulling the knitting after Jess. The knitting stopped. Jess went through the hedge again. Then he stopped. The woolly monster was no longer after him. Jess lay down on the grass until he felt better. Then he gave himself a wash.

Pat stroked Jess, to cheer him up.

Katy came and
gave Jess a cuddle.

Tom brought him
a saucer of cream.

When Miss Hubbard saw her knitting, she was so cross that she stamped her foot and said, "Just look what a mess that cat's made of my knitting! I'll never get it untangled; never in all this world!"

Oh, dear, it was in a mess! It had collected bits of grass and leaves and twigs. There were bits of hen-food in it. It was sopping wet from the duck-pond.

Pat and Peter and Ted all came to help.

They pulled and pushed that knitting.
They twisted and turned that knitting.
They squeezed the water out and shook that knitting dry.

There were arms and fingers everywhere. Soon, they got themselves nearly as tangled as the knitting. And they were nearly as cross as Miss Hubbard herself. Because, when they had finished, Miss Hubbard said, "It's worse than ever!"

"Oh, dear," said Pat, "it is!"

Then Miss Hubbard picked up the tangled mess, and dropped it into Mrs. Pottage's dustbin.

"And *that's* the end of my new jumper," she said.

Just then, Mrs. Pottage came out of her house, with a big plastic bag in her hands.

"I've just remembered," she said. "There's this wool that I bought in Pencaster, and I never got round to making anything with it. I'm sure I'll not have time, what with baby Paul and everything. I was wondering if . . . well . . . do you like purple, Miss Hubbard?"

"Oh, what *lovely* wool," said Miss Hubbard. "And purple's my favourite colour."

"Do have it, then," said Mrs. Pottage. "You're very welcome."

"Well," said Miss Hubbard, "I do think I like it better than that old orange stuff. Yes, I like it much better. It'll go with my new skirt. Well, then, I will accept your kind offer."

Miss Hubbard was so pleased with her new wool, that she forgot about being cross, and began to smile and chat with everyone.

Then Mrs. Pottage brought tea and cakes, and they all felt much better. It was like a garden party.

But, when Jess came to look at Miss Hubbard's bag of wool, she said, "Oh, *shoooooo*, you naughty cat!"

And she said to Pat, "If that cat comes near my knitting again, I'll. . . ."

"No fear of that," said Pat. "He had such a fright that he'll *never* go near knitting again. You can be sure of that. And I'm sorry he made such a mess. I know he didn't mean any harm. He's not really a naughty cat. He was only running for his life."

“Well, then, I’ll forgive him,” said Miss Hubbard. “Come on, Jess. I’m not cross with you now.”

And she gave Jess a stroke, to show that she meant it.

"I'd better be on my way," said Pat. "Come on, Jess. Cheerio, everybody!"

Pat was right. Jess never went near a *clickety-click* mouse again. He kept to the kind that go *squeak*.